W9-BQU-569

*Understanding the Elements of the Periodic Table*™

# CHLORINE

Linda Saucerman

rosen publishing's
rosen
central®

New York

*To the Amazing Steve and Matthew!*

Published in 2008 by The Rosen Publishing Group, Inc.
29 East 21st Street, New York, NY 10010

First Edition

**Library of Congress Cataloging-in-Publication Data**

Saucerman, Linda.
Chlorine / Linda Saucerman.—1st ed.
p. cm.—(Understanding the elements of the periodic table)
Includes bibliographical references and index.
ISBN-13: 978-1-4042-1962-5
ISBN-10: 1-4042-1962-5
1. Chlorine—Juvenile literature. 2. Periodic law—Tables—Juvenile literature.
I. Title.
QD181.C5S26 2007
546'.732—dc22

2007000909

*Manufactured in China*

**On the cover:** Chlorine's square on the periodic table of elements. Inset: the subatomic structure of a chlorine atom.

# Contents

# Introduction

With its bright white head and intense yellow eyes, the bald eagle is the symbol of strength and freedom for the United States of America. The founders of this country chose the bald eagle as the national symbol because it lives only in North America, where the United States is located. But what would it mean to Americans if the bald eagle no longer existed? It may seem like a silly question, but we almost found out what life would be like without our national bird.

In 1782, when the bald eagle became the symbol for the United States, more than 100,000 bald eagles lived throughout the country. In the 1800s, the area that would later become the state of Alaska was home to more than 200,000 bald eagles. But in the 1960s, bald eagles and other raptors, or hunting birds, began to disappear. No one knew why.

The first clue to the mystery was found in the nests the eagles built. These nests, which can measure almost twenty feet across, sheltered the eagles' eggs. Like all eggs, these were fragile. But scientists realized that the bald eagle eggs were even more fragile than they should have been. When the adult eagles sat on the eggs to keep them warm, the shells would break, and the baby eagles would die. All over the country, the eggshells of bald eagles and other raptors were cracking open too soon.

If the scientists wanted to save the bald eagle from dying out completely, they knew they had to find out quickly why the eggshells were so thin. The

Majestic bald eagles have a wingspan of up to eight feet (2.4 meters). They use their sharp talons to snatch fish from rivers and lakes.

scientists started by examining the broken eggs and the bodies of dead eagles. Inside of eagles' bodies, they kept finding the same chemical: dichloro-diphenyl-trichloroethane, or DDT. As the "chloro-" in the name indicates, this chemical contains chlorine.

It was odd that the scientists found this chemical in eagles and their eggs. Chemical companies manufactured DDT as a pesticide, or bug killer. During World War II (1939–1945), the military sprayed DDT in and around rivers, streams, and wetlands to kill disease-spreading mosquitoes. However, people soon realized that DDT killed not only mosquitoes, but nearly every other type of insect that came in contact with it. So, throughout the 1950s, people across the country used DDT to kill all sorts of pests. Huge amounts of the chemical were sprayed on large farm fields as well as in small backyard gardens.

The problem is that DDT does not break apart in water. This means that when it rains, DDT seeps into the water in the ground or flows to nearby streams, rivers, lakes, and eventually the oceans. The U.S. Fish and Wildlife Service says that from the 1940s through the 1970s, millions of pounds of DDT entered the oceans surrounding North America.

Once the DDT was in the water, it was absorbed into the flesh of fish and other animals living in the water. When eagles and other birds ate the fish that were contaminated with DDT, these birds became contaminated, too.

In 1958, a scientist named Rachel Carson began looking at how DDT affected birds and other living things, including humans. For more than four years, she studied everything she could about DDT. Using her research, she wrote a book called *Silent Spring*. Her book warned that the chlorine-based pesticide was causing the death of thousands of animals and possibly making people sick, too. *Silent Spring* was featured in newspapers and magazines as well as on television news, and people all over the country started questioning whether DDT was safe to use.

By 1963, only about 800 bald eagles were left in the United States outside of Alaska. Fortunately, Americans acted fast to save their beloved bird. The government banned all uses of DDT in the United States. (It was still used elsewhere, however.) In addition, the bald eagle was listed as an endangered species, which assisted the government in making laws and granting money to scientists. The scientists then used the money and the new laws to start bald eagle protection programs. Their efforts succeeded in changing the fate of the great American symbol. Today, nearly 12,000 bald eagles live in the lower forty-eight states, and thousands more live in Alaska.

# Chapter One
# Chlorine's Mistaken Identity

**P**esticides such as DDT and other chemicals made from chlorine can be harmful to people and animals. But chlorine is not always dangerous. In fact, many beneficial, or useful, chlorine-containing substances are found in nature.

## Elements and Compounds

Chlorine is an element. Elements are single substances that cannot become different substances through physical or chemical changes. The element iron (Fe), for example, can be made into a nail. If you cut the iron nail in half, it is still the element iron. If you continue to cut the nail until it is so small that you can barely see it, you are still going to be holding the element iron. Even if you were able to cut the nail down to the size of a single atom, you would still have the element iron. (We'll learn more about atoms later.)

However, if you were able to combine the iron atom with an atom of another element, then it would form a compound. Compounds occur when two or more different elements combine. Rust, for example, is a compound made of the elements iron and oxygen (O).

In nature, chlorine does not exist in a pure elemental form. It exists only in compounds. In fact, chlorine was first discovered by a scientist who was experimenting with various compounds.

# Chlorine Is Discovered

In 1774, Swedish chemist Carl Wilhelm Scheele (1742–1786) mixed a shiny mineral with a liquid compound he called spiritus salis. All of a sudden, a very sharp-smelling, greenish-yellow gas started to pour forth from the mixture. Scheele wrote in his notes that the experiment created a "suffocating smell, which was most oppressive to the lungs."

Scheele continued to experiment with this gas. He observed that it dissolved some metals and caused red flower petals to turn white. But in spite of the gas's special properties, Scheele was not sure whether he had identified a new element. He thought the mysterious substance might be a compound containing the element oxygen.

In 1810, more than thirty years later, a young English chemist named Humphry Davy (1778–1829) began conducting tests on the gas. Davy wanted to test Scheele's theory to see whether the gas contained oxygen. He tried over and over to extract, or pull out, oxygen from the gas, but he never could do it. After many more tests, Davy realized that the gas was not a compound of oxygen at all. In fact, it was not even a compound—it was an element! Because of the gas's color, Davy

This is a statue of chemist Carl Wilhelm Scheele. It was erected in Stockholm, Sweden, to honor the great Swedish chemist.

## Sir Humphry Davy

In addition to proving that chlorine was a single element, Humphry Davy identified the elements potassium (K), sodium (Na), magnesium (Mg), calcium (Ca), strontium (Sr), barium (Ba), and iodine (I). He also invented a special helmet lamp for coal miners. His discoveries made him popular with other scientists, and even regular English people of the 1800s knew his name.

By the time he was thirty-four years old, Humphry Davy was such a successful scientist that the British royal family decided to make him a knight. He then became known as Sir Humphry Davy. Unfortunately for Davy, all the scientific experiments and all the glory he received came at a price. In 1810, the same year he identified chlorine as an element, a mixture of chemicals in Davy's lab exploded and temporarily blinded him. Eventually, the long years of exposure to chemicals caused him to become very sick, and he died when he was only fifty-one years old. Some say that Davy died in the name of science.

named the element "chlorine," from the Greek word *chloros*, meaning "greenish yellow."

# Elements and Atoms

In addition to its color and strong odor, chlorine has other properties that make it different from the rest of the elements. In fact, no two elements are exactly alike. Individual elements are different because the atoms they are made of are different.

This bottle contains greenish-yellow chlorine gas. Exposure to chlorine in this form can damage the eyes, skin, and lungs.

Atoms are the basic building blocks of all matter. The atoms of an element combine with other atoms to form molecules. Chlorine atoms combine to create chlorine molecules. During Scheele's and Davy's experiments with chlorine, they saw a greenish-yellow gas. This gas is made up of diatomic chlorine molecules. (*Diatomic* means "containing two atoms.") These are molecules that contain two chlorine atoms. In chemical formulas that contain chlorine, you often see the diatomic form of chlorine written as $Cl_2$.

Until the twentieth century, the atom was the smallest known physical structure. Then physicists discovered that atoms are made up of even smaller parts, subatomic particles called protons, neutrons, and electrons. They also discovered that atoms were held together by the electromagnetic attraction between subatomic particles. Protons have a positive electric charge; electrons have a negative electric charge. Neutrons, as their name indicates, are neutral, meaning they have no charge.

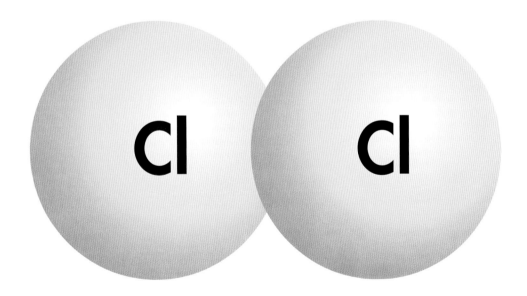

Two atoms join together to create a diatomic molecule. Chlorine gas is made up of diatomic chlorine molecules, one of which is modeled here.

# Subatomic Particles

The protons, neutrons, and electrons in all atoms are alike. It is the number and arrangement of these subatomic particles that make an atom of one element different from the atoms of all other elements. All atoms have a core called a nucleus. The protons and neutrons are found inside this nucleus. Chlorine atoms, and only chlorine atoms, have seventeen protons. The number of protons in an atom is called the atomic number, so chlorine's atomic number is 17. Most chlorine atoms found in nature (about 75 percent) have eighteen neutrons, while some (about 25 percent) contain twenty neutrons. All chlorine atoms have seventeen electrons.

Elements in the periodic table (see pages 38–39) are organized according to their atomic numbers, or the number of protons in their nuclei. Each element has its own atomic number. The element with the lowest atomic number (hydrogen, with an atomic number of 1) is located in the upper left-hand corner of the table. Presently, the element with the highest atomic number (ununhexium, atomic number 116) is located in the lower right-hand corner. Chlorine's seventeen protons make it the seventeenth element on the periodic table.

An atom's electrons move around in shells that are located outside of the nucleus. An atom can have just one shell, or it can have up to seven shells.

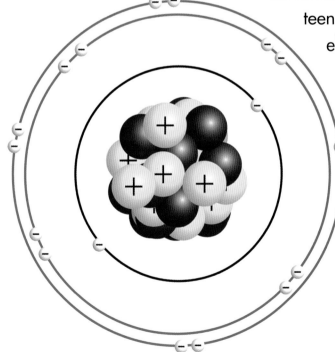

A chlorine atom has seventeen electrons *(smaller light-blue spheres)*. The nucleus of the chlorine atom contains its protons *(yellow spheres)* and neutrons *(brown spheres)*.

For all elements, the rules for the shells are the same: The first shell can hold two electrons, and the second shell can hold up to eight electrons. The third shell can hold thirty-two electrons, and the higher shells can hold even more. A chlorine atom has three shells. It has two electrons in its first shell, eight in its second, and seven in its third. Add these numbers, and you'll see that chlorine has seventeen total electrons.

The number of electrons in an atom's outer shell determines whether the atom is reactive or not reactive. For chlorine, its seven electrons in its outer shell make it very reactive with other elements. (You'll learn more about reactivity in chapter 2.) It was chlorine's ability to react with other elements that interested Scheele and Davy in the late 1700s and early 1800s. In the later 1800s, chlorine continued to inspire other scientists, including a chemist who forever changed how we look at elements.

# Chapter Two
# Chlorine Comes to the Table

In the 1860s, a young Russian chemist named Dmitry Mendeleyev stopped at an enormous salt mine in Poland. He was fascinated by all the elements found in the mine, including chlorine, sodium, bromine (Br), and potassium. He wondered how all these elements could be in the same mine and how they behaved and reacted with each other. He walked away from the mine not knowing the answers to his questions, but he continued to think about them.

Several years later, Mendeleyev was teaching chemistry at the University of St. Petersburg in Russia. He wanted to create a better way for his students to study the elements, so he began thinking again about the properties of all the different elements. For instance, he considered the atomic mass, or weight, of each known element. He created individual cards for each element and then arranged them in a horizontal row, according to their atomic mass. Mendeleyev knew the weights of hydrogen (the lightest) through uranium (the heaviest known at the time) and placed them accordingly. He knew that the elements had some predictable properties, so he split up the rows so that elements with similar properties fell into the same columns. When arranged like this, his chart showed repeating patterns, or periods, among the properties of the elements. This new chart, which he published in 1869, became known as the periodic table of elements. Mendeleyev's chart evolved into the periodic table we know today.

но въ ней, мнѣ кажется, уже ясно выражается примѣнимость выставляемаго мною начала ко всей совокупности элементовъ, пай которыхъ извѣстенъ съ достовѣрностію. На этотъ разъ я и желалъ преимущественно найдти общую систему элементовъ. Вотъ этотъ опытъ:

```
                              Ti=50      Zr=90    ?=180.
                              V=51       Nb=94    Ta=182.
                              Cr=52      Mo=96    W=186.
                              Mn=55      Rh=104,4 Pt=197,4
                              Fe=56      Ru=104,4 Ir=198.
                          Ni=Co=59       Pl=106,6 Os=199.
 H=1                          Cu=63,4     Ag=108  Hg=200.
        Be=9,4     Mg=24      Zn=65,2     Cd=112
        B=11       Al=27,4    ?=68        Ur=116  Au=197?
        C=12       Si=28      ?=70        Sn=118
        N=14       P=31       As=75       Sb=122  Bi=210
        O=16       S=32       Se=79,4     Te=128?
        F=19       Cl=35,5    Br=80       I=127
 Li=7   Na=23      K=39       Rb=85,4     Cs=133  Tl=204
                   Ca=40      Sr=87,6     Ba=137  Pb=207.
                   ?=45       Ce=92
                   ?Er=56     La=94
                   ?Yt=60     Di=95
                   ?In=75,6   Th=118?
```

а потому приходится въ разныхъ рядахъ имѣть различное измѣненіе разностей, чего нѣтъ въ главныхъ числахъ предлагаемой таблицы. Или же придется предполагать при составленіи системы очень много недостающихъ членовъ. То и другое мало выгодно. Мнѣ кажется притомъ, наиболѣе естественнымъ составить кубическую систему (предлагаемая есть плоскостная), но и попытки для ея образованія не повели къ надлежащимъ результатамъ. Слѣдующія двѣ попытки могутъ показать то разнообразіе сопоставленій, какое возможно при допущеніи основнаго начала, высказаннаго въ этой статьѣ.

| Li | Na | K | Cu | Rb | Ag | Cs | — | Tl |
|----|----|----|----|----|----|----|----|----|
| 7 | 23 | 39 | 63,4 | 85,4 | 108 | 133 | | 204 |
| Be | Mg | Ca | Zn | Sr | Cd | Ba | — | Pb |
| B | Al | — | — | — | Ur | — | — | Bi? |
| C | Si | Ti | — | Zr | Sn | — | — | — |
| N | P | V | As | Nb | Sb | — | Ta | — |
| O | S | — | Se | — | Te | — | W | — |
| F | Cl | — | Br | — | J | — | — | — |
| 19 | 35,5 | 58 | 80 | 190 | 127 | 160 | 190 | 220. |

Mendeleyev's original periodic table *(above)* listed the elements by increasing atomic weight. Chlorine (Cl) is in the third row from the left, with its atomic weight written as 35,5.

# Chlorine  Snapshot

17 Cl 35

| | |
|---|---|
| Chemical Symbol: | Cl |
| Classification: | Nonmetal |
| Properties: | Poisonous, greenish-yellow, water-soluble gas; highly reactive; occurs only in compounds in nature; not combustible but will enable other elements to catch fire (oxidizing agent) |
| Discovered by: | Carl Wilhelm Scheele in 1774; confirmed as an element in 1810 by Sir Humphry Davy |
| Atomic Number: | 17 |
| Atomic Weight: | 35.453 amu |
| Protons: | 17 |
| Electrons: | 17 |
| Neutrons: | 18 (75 percent); 20 (25 percent) |
| State of Matter at 68° Fahrenheit (20° Celsius): | Gas |
| Melting Point: | −150.7°F (−101.5°C) |
| Boiling Point: | −30.28°F (−34.6°C) |
| Commonly Found: | In seawater and Earth's crust |

# Changes in the Periodic Table

In January 2004, a team of American and Russian scientists announced they had created two new elements: ununtrium (Uut) and ununpentium (Uup). Within a few seconds of producing Uut and Uup, the scientists observed that the elements started to break down, or decay. In the blink of an eye, Uut and Uup had quickly changed from new elements into elements that were already known to exist.

Even though the scientists observed Uut and Uup, these elements were not automatically added to the periodic table. Instead, they have been temporarily placed in the gaps at the bottom of the periodic table. Uut is element 113, and Uup is element 115. Other scientists are attempting to repeat the creation of these two hefty elements to be sure that the original announcements were correct. If more tests confirm that Uut and Uup really are reproducible elements, they will eventually get new names and permanent spots on the table.

Uut has an atomic weight of 284, and Uup has an atomic weight of 288. The relatively enormous atomic weights of these new elements led scientists to describe them as "superheavies."

Scientists create "super-heavy" elements under extremely specific conditions in the lab. To observe and measure these elements, scientists have to use very precise instruments.

Being quite astute, Mendeleyev left empty spaces in his table where no element with suitable properties was known. Since 1869, many of the elements predicted by Mendeleyev have been discovered and added to the table.

# Setting the Table: Periods

The modern periodic table takes Mendeleyev's idea and makes it just a little easier to understand. The original version arranged the elements according to weight, or atomic mass. Today's version arranges the elements by atomic number, which represents the number of protons in the nucleus of the atom. Like Mendeleyev's table, the periodic table we use today has horizontal rows called periods. In each period, the elements are arranged from the least to greatest atomic number, reading from left to right. You'll find chlorine in the third period, on the right-hand side of the periodic table. (See periodic table on pages 38–39.)

# Setting the Table: Groups

In addition to organizing elements by periods, the periodic table arranges elements in groups. An element is assigned a group based on its chemical properties. Many of these properties are related to the number of electrons in the outermost shell of the element's atom.

In one system, each group is assigned a number, 1 through 18, which appears above its column in the table. In a different system, the groups are identified by a Roman numeral and a letter, either A or B. Some tables, like the one in this book, include both labels. Elements in the A groups are known as representative elements. Chlorine is in an A group. Elements in the B groups, such as iron and copper (Cu), are all classified as metals.

The elements within a group sometimes are referred to as a family of elements. Chlorine and the other elements belonging to group 17 (or VIIA)

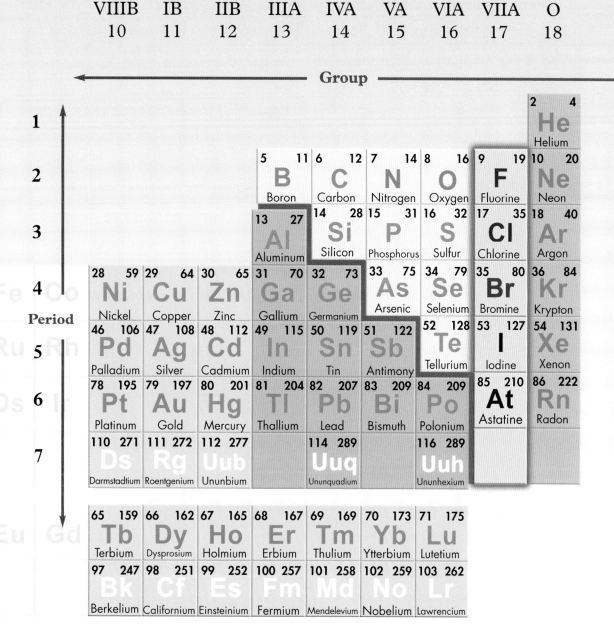

| | VIIIB 10 | IB 11 | IIB 12 | IIIA 13 | IVA 14 | VA 15 | VIA 16 | VIIA 17 | O 18 |

**Group** →

**Period**

This is the right side of the periodic table. The halogen group (Group VIIA/Group 17) is highlighted. Chlorine is located in the second row of the halogen group. The number in the upper left-hand corner of chlorine's square is the element's atomic number, or number of protons. The number in the upper right-hand corner shows the element's approximate atomic weight.

make up a family known as the halogens. *Halogens* means "salt formers." In chemical terms, a salt is formed when a metal atom replaces a hydrogen atom in an acid compound. Table salt, for example, is a salt called sodium chloride (NaCl). It is formed when the metal sodium (Na) replaces the hydrogen (H) in hydrochloric acid (HCl).

The first element in group 17 is fluorine (F), the most reactive element in the group. Reactive means that it will easily combine with other elements. Chlorine, which is also very reactive, is the second halogen. The other halogens are bromine, iodine, and astatine (At).

The halogens are considered nonmetals. Elements that are nonmetals are not good electrical conductors. In other words, nonmetals do not conduct, or carry, electricity very well. Another property of some non-metals is that they are not very malleable, meaning they are not easily shaped into something else. Nonmetals can exist as gases like chlorine and as solids like sulfur (S).

# Chapter Three
# Chlorine Compounds

The chemical behavior of atoms largely depends on electric charges. In particular, it is the arrangement of the negatively charged electrons that determines how elements react with one another. Do you remember that electrons circulate in shells? The number of electrons in an atom's outermost shell is crucial to its chemical behavior, for it is these electrons that allow an atom to create bonds with other atoms. Chemical bonds are either covalent or ionic.

## Chlorine and Covalent Bonds

In a chlorine atom, seven of its seventeen total electrons are in its outermost (third) electron shell. The outermost shell sometimes is called the valence shell, so the seven electrons in it are called valence electrons. Chlorine's valence electrons allow it to form covalent bonds, which result when atoms share electrons. Hydrogen chloride (HCl), for example, is a molecule made up of one hydrogen atom and one chlorine atom. Hydrogen has one electron in its outer shell, which it tends to share with other atoms. Chlorine has seven electrons in its outer shell. When chlorine and hydrogen combine, hydrogen shares its one electron with chlorine. Chlorine then has eight electrons in its outer shell. This fills chlorine's outer shell, giving

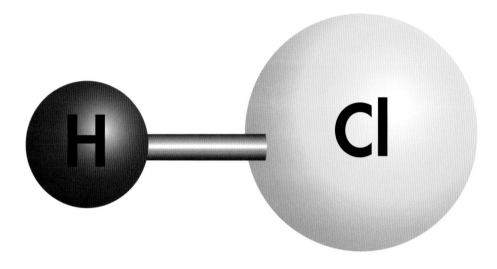

This diagram shows the chemical bond in a molecule of hydrogen chloride. The hydrogen atom (H) and the chlorine atom (Cl) share an electron to create a covalent bond.

it a stable electron arrangement. At the same time, chlorine shares one of its electrons with the hydrogen atom. Hydrogen then has two electrons in its outer shell, making it full, too. By sharing electrons, both atoms get stable, filled outer shells.

Hydrogen chloride is an important molecule. Without it, you wouldn't be able to digest the food you eat. Inside your stomach is a weak form of hydrochloric acid, which is hydrogen chloride dissolved in water. The hydrochloric acid in your stomach breaks down food so that your body can absorb the proteins and other nutrients. This gives you energy to read this book, ride your bike . . . to live! Hydrogen chloride is just one of the many compounds of chlorine that our bodies rely on.

## Radioactive Chlorine

Isotopes are atoms of an element that have the same number of protons but a different number of neutrons. This means isotopes have the same atomic number but a different atomic weight. Some isotopes occur naturally, and others are created by scientists in laboratories under specific conditions. Chlorine has nine different isotopes, seven of which are radioactive. A radioactive isotope is one that breaks down and emits, or gives off, some type of radiation. This radiation can be measured by special instruments.

Chlorine-36 (also written as 36Cl) is a radioactive isotope formed naturally when cosmic radiation from the solar system reacts with Earth's atmosphere. Tiny amounts of chlorine-36 are found in our atmosphere as well as on the moon and on Mars. Scientists have discovered that chlorine-36 has a half-life of about 300,000 years. This means it will take about that long for half of this element to decay, or break down, into a different element. When archaeologists, geologists, and other scientists are studying the ocean or something else that is very old, they sometimes look for chlorine-36. If it is present, then they can measure the isotope's radioactivity to figure out how old the thing is.

# Chlorine and Ionic Bonds

If you've ever gone swimming in the ocean, you have been in the water with the compound sodium chloride (NaCl). This combination of sodium and chlorine gives seawater its salty taste. In fact, sodium chloride is the chemical name for table salt, the seasoning you sprinkle on your food.

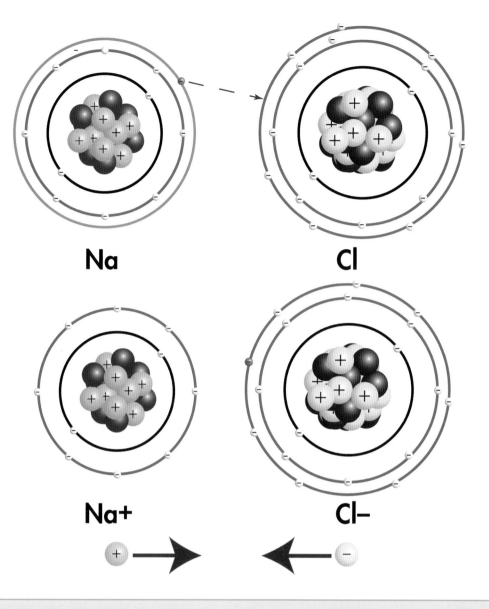

Na

Cl

Na+

Cl−

A molecule of sodium chloride is held together by an ionic bond. To create the bond, a sodium atom (Na) gives up the electron in its outer shell to a chlorine atom *(top)*. The transfer of a negative electron gives sodium a positive charge (+) and chlorine a negative charge (–) *(bottom)*. The opposite electrical charges hold the atoms together.

You know that covalent bonds occur when atoms share one or more electrons. In the bond that holds together sodium chloride, one of the atoms donates one or more electrons to another element.

How does this type of bond work? Sodium has one electron in its outermost shell. Under the right conditions, the neutrally charged sodium atom gives up this electron when it comes together with a chlorine atom. When the sodium atom loses an electron, it is left with a positive charge. On the other hand, a chlorine atom that gains an electron from sodium becomes negatively charged. As a result of the transfer of electrons, the attraction between the positive sodium and the negative chlorine holds the two atoms together. Charged atoms are called ions, so this attraction is called an ionic bond.

## Undoing Ionic Bonds

So, sodium chloride is an ionic compound made of sodium and chlorine. Scientists discovered that sodium chloride from seawater can be separated to produce chlorine gas. One common way this is done is by passing electricity through a container of seawater. This method, called electrolysis, separates the chloride ion atoms from the sodium ions.

How is this possible? The flow of electricity takes the electron away from the chloride ion and gives it back to the sodium ion. When electrons are removed, the chloride ions become chlorine atoms, which are released from the seawater as a gas. There are laboratories around the world that have huge vats, or tubs, of salt water that get zapped with electricity so that scientists can then collect the chlorine gas that is released.

## Salt of the Earth

In addition to electrolysis, scientists use the remains of ancient oceans to produce chlorine. Deep inside the earth are giant pillars of salt called salt domes. These salt domes are made from the same salt that was in the oceans where dinosaurs once swam. As the ocean water evaporated, the salt from the seawater was left behind, creating thick salt beds or salt flats. Over millions of years, these salt flats were covered by layers of sediment, dirt, and rock, and ended up buried deep underground.

This huge chemical plant is using electrolysis to separate chlorine gas from brine, or salt water. Electrolysis is very efficient, as little chlorine is lost in the process.

Sometimes this ancient salt appears on the earth's surface when it rises up through the groundwater and forms brine pools. (Brine is another way to describe salt water.) When you see these brine pools far from the ocean, you know that an ancient salt bed must be underground. The underground salt can be mined by digging. Another method of collection is called solution mining. This requires long pipes to be inserted deep into the ground. One pipe pushes water into the ground until it reaches the salt. The salt and water then get mixed together, dissolving the salt and creating brine. Another pipe with a pump sucks this salty mixture, or solution, up to the earth's surface. The water then is evaporated from the solution, leaving behind salt.

A large construction crane is used to dig up salt on this "salt farm" in China. The bags you see are filled with the harvested salt.

Evaporation alone can be used to gather salt, too. In areas near seawater, like California, there are large ponds of salt water that have formed naturally or have been created by humans. A system of small dams helps to keep this salty water in one place so that the sun and wind can evaporate the water. The salt that is left behind is then harvested, more salt water is added, and the cycle starts all over again.

The methods described here produce the sodium chloride that is made into salt to season your food or chlorine to whiten your socks. In 2004, approximately 220 million tons of salt were produced in the world. Of that amount, the United States produced the most—more than fifty million tons.

# Chapter Four
# Killer Chlorine

Chlorine is poisonous and can be deadly. During World War I, German chemists invented ways for chlorine gas to be used as a weapon. The gas was pumped directly onto the battlefield using tanks and hoses, or it was delivered from above using special artillery shells. Before the chlorine was released, German soldiers put on gas masks, which protected them from inhaling it. With the help of the wind, the greenish-yellow gas would waft over the enemy trenches. Being denser than air, the cloud of chlorine gas hovered near the surface. Just like the suffocating gas that Scheele and Davy experienced, this gas immediately started to damage the throats, lungs, and eyes of unprotected soldiers. Many were injured or killed.

Other chlorine-based gases, such as deadly mustard gas, were used by many countries in World War II. (As recently as 2007, insurgents in Iraq used chlorine gas as a weapon of terror.) These gases had the ability to kill people almost instantly, or they could kill very slowly and painfully. Once released, they also poisoned birds, fish, and other animals that were unlucky enough to be in the area. In 1925, a mere ten years after chlorine gas was first used as a weapon of war, more than 100 nations signed on to the Geneva Protocol. This agreement banned the use of "asphyxiating gas" and other chemical weapons.

In World War I, chlorine was turned into a fearsome weapon. These French soldiers are wearing goggles and face masks to protect themselves from chlorine gas attacks launched by the Germans.

# CFCs

Unfortunately, DDT and chlorine gases aren't the only ways that humans have tainted the environment with chlorine. Chlorofluorocarbons, or CFCs, are useful synthetic (manufactured) compounds made from chlorine, carbon, and fluorine. One type of CFC was found to be a very good coolant, so it was widely used in refrigerators and air conditioners. CFCs in liquid form could be added to spray cans to act as a propellant for products such as air deodorizers and hairspray. But in the 1970s, scientists started to realize that CFCs were depleting, or eating away at, the ozone layer

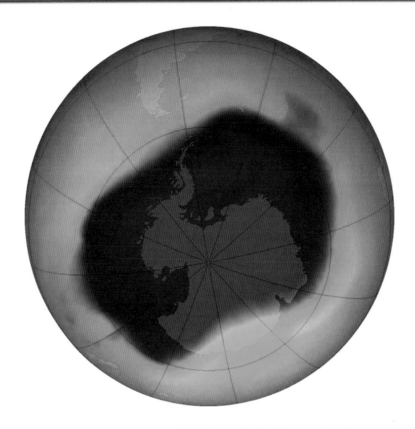

This satellite image from 2006 shows the ozone hole over Antarctica, at the South Pole. In the blue and purple areas, the amounts of UV rays from the sun are the most powerful.

that surrounds Earth. This layer of the atmosphere protects us from the sun's ultraviolet (UV) rays, which can damage eyes and cause skin cancer.

The ozone layer is made up of ozone molecules ($O_3$). When CFCs encounter ozone molecules, they change those ozone molecules into a form of chlorine. This new form of chlorine then reacts with other ozone molecules and changes them, too. So a single CFC molecule can ultimately destroy thousands of ozone molecules. When it became clear what was happening in the atmosphere, governments around the world began passing laws to ban the use of CFCs. (The United States completely phased out the production of CFCs in 1996.) Laws have helped to slow the damage to the ozone layer, but they can't reverse the harm that already has been done.

# PCBs

Polychlorinated biphenyls (PCBs) are another class of chlorine compounds that has harmed the environment. Beginning in 1929, these chemicals were used in everything from mascara to machinery. Similar to CFCs, PCBs were used to keep things cool and dissolve mixtures, but PCBs also had many other uses. In fact, nearly every manufacturer across the globe used PCBs.

Unfortunately, as with CFCs, the miracle of PCBs was too good to be true. In the late 1970s, scientists discovered that PCBs caused cancer. Even worse, PCBs were hard to remove from the environment. So even if the harmful compounds were no longer produced, the PCBs already in the ground and the water could still cause cancer in people and animals. Just like DDT, PCBs got into the rivers, streams, and lakes in America and started to make bald eagles sick. By 1977, the U.S. government banned the domestic production of PCBs.

# Carbon Tetrachloride

At one time, even your local dry cleaner used a dangerous chlorine compound. Carbon tetrachloride, or $CCl_4$ is a solvent, which means it can dissolve other substances. $CCl_4$ is so strong it can dissolve grease and oil. Dry-cleaning businesses used it to clean clothes that were too delicate to be washed with soap and water. Sometimes this solvent wasn't stored or disposed of properly, so it started to ooze into the drinking water supply. Think about how powerful this solvent has to be to break down grease. Then think about how delicate your liver, kidneys, and other organs are! More people and the environment were exposed to $CCl_4$, and scientists soon determined that it could be a deadly combination. Dry cleaners now use more environmentally safe cleaners.

# Chapter Five
# Kudos to Chlorine

**W**hile some chlorine compounds are too dangerous to be used, there are many chlorine compounds that are beneficial to humans. For example, chlorine is combined with other elements to create some kinds of plastic. Look around your house and you will find plastic in nearly every room. There are probably chlorine-containing plastic trash bags in your kitchen, plastic pipes attached to your bathroom sink, and a plastic remote control for your television.

## Clean with Chlorine

Look in the laundry room of your house and you'll find chlorine—in bleach. Sodium hypochlorite (NaOCl), or bleach, is a compound made from one atom of sodium, one atom of oxygen, and one atom of chlorine. Do you remember how the chemist Carl Wilhelm Scheele discovered that chlorine gas would make red flower petals turn white? The bleach you buy at the grocery store can have the same effect. Bleach is used on dirty clothing to whiten it. Bleach may help to get your socks and underwear nice and white, but you still have to be careful when you use it. It can easily get onto clothing that you don't want to whiten, and then you end up with a bleach spot. If you get bleach on your skin, it can burn. If bleach gets in your eyes, it can blind you.

A simple experiment shows the whitening power of bleach. Three flasks contain grape juice, cranberry juice, and tomato juice (1). A small amount of bleach (sodium hypochlorite) is added to each flask (2). Almost immediately, the chemical action of the bleach turns the juices to a much lighter color (3).

# Chlorine as Disinfectant

If you've ever gone to a swimming pool, you've come into contact with sodium hypochlorite there, too. Bleach is added to swimming pools to help prevent bacteria and algae from growing. If bleach were not added to a pool, clumps of green algae would begin to grow and float around inside it. It would be more like swimming in a pond!

Green algae are made up of living cells. When these cells come into contact with the sodium hypochlorite, a chemical reaction takes place. During the reaction, chlorine atoms replace the original atoms in the proteins of the cell membranes. This causes a change in the shape of the membranes and kills the algae.

You have to be careful when using bleach in a pool. Like algae, you also are made up of living cells. If you add too much bleach to the pool, it can harm your cells, causing your eyes and skin to feel itchy and dry.

Disinfectant bleach is added to drinking water. Humans can suffer and even die when they drink water that has certain bacteria floating in it. In the early 1900s, for example, more than 25,000 people died from typhoid fever, a disease caused by bacteria. To stop the spread of disease, chlorine was added to drinking water. The Chlorine Chemistry Council says that 98 percent of drinking water in the United States now has chlorine added to it, and now hardly anyone in America dies from typhoid fever anymore. In other countries, however, deadly bacteria thrive in some sources of drinking water. Governments and organizations are continuing to work together to bring chlorinated water to poorer nations.

# Craving Chlorine

Humans have used sodium chloride (table salt) for thousands of years. In fact, some of the earliest books ever written tell about people using salt. In the "caveman kitchen," salt was used to prepare food so that it would

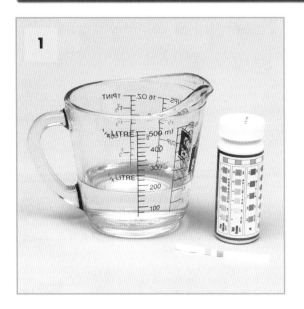

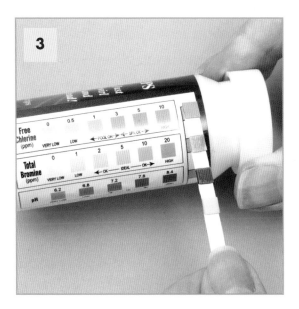

Testing kits (1) are an easy way to measure chlorine in pool water. A chemically treated test strip is dipped into a water sample (2). After a minute, the colors on the strip are compared to a key (3). According to the key, the ideal chlorine content is between 1 and 3 parts per million (ppm). However, this sample turned the strip a light-blue color, which means the water has at least 10 ppm of chlorine. This swimming-pool water has too much chlorine.

last longer. When fish or meat is covered in salt, the salt draws moisture out of it. Without a moist environment, mold and other bacteria cannot grow, and so the meat does not spoil. Preserving food by salting is still done today.

Salt is used to add extra flavor to foods. One of the reasons why we like the taste of salt is because we need it in order to be healthy. According to the Salt Institute, we all need about .28 percent of salt in our bodies to stay healthy. So, having salt in your diet helps to keep the natural chemical balance inside your body. However, too much in your diet can be a bad thing. An excess of salt can cause heart problems and other illnesses.

# Rocky Roads

Sodium chloride in its mineral form, called halite or rock salt, is used to clear roads of ice and snow. For this reason, it also is called road salt. If you live in an area that has harsh winter weather, you'll often see trucks spreading road salt. Vehicles' tires crush the solid NaCl crystals, which then combine with liquid water ($H_2O$) in the ice and snow. This lowers the freezing point of the water, causing the snow and ice to melt.

Like other chlorine compounds, road salt must be used with caution. Scientists have found that it pollutes rivers, lakes, and even the oceans. Rain washes the road salt off the roads, and it eventually flows to the nearest body of water. Excessive amounts of road salt harms the plants and animals that live in the delicate water ecosystems. Lake Ontario is one body of water that has high levels of chlorine from the road salt that flows into it after heavy rain. This freshwater lake sits between the United States and Canada. Both countries are working together to reduce the amount of road salt used on highways and roads near Lake Ontario.

Another chlorine compound, calcium chloride ($CaCl_2$), is used to melt ice and snow. It is less harmful to plants than sodium chloride but still causes problems in water ecosystems.

# Chlorine: In Conclusion

From the ozone layer to the oceans, the dangers of chlorine compounds seem to be everywhere. However, chlorine also is at work inside your stomach, and it is a major reason why you will probably never get sick

Halite, a form of sodium chloride (NaCl), is a common mineral. Huge deposits of halite sit under Detroit and Cleveland. Appropriately named Salt Lake City, Utah, is the site of another large halite deposit.

from water-borne bacteria. From industry and manufacturing to food preparation and water decontamination, the benefits of chlorine and its compounds guarantee that the element will continue to be used for a long time.

# The Periodic Table of Elements

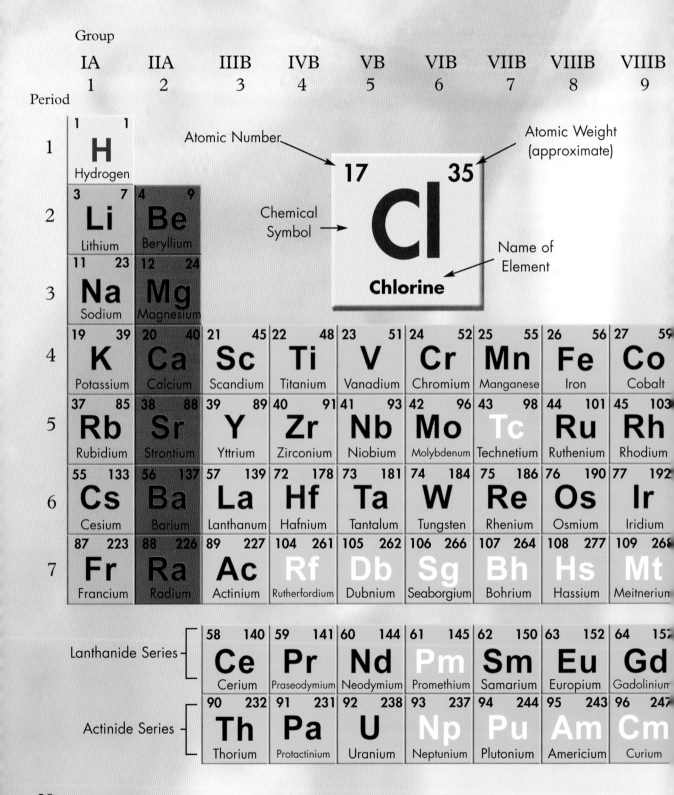

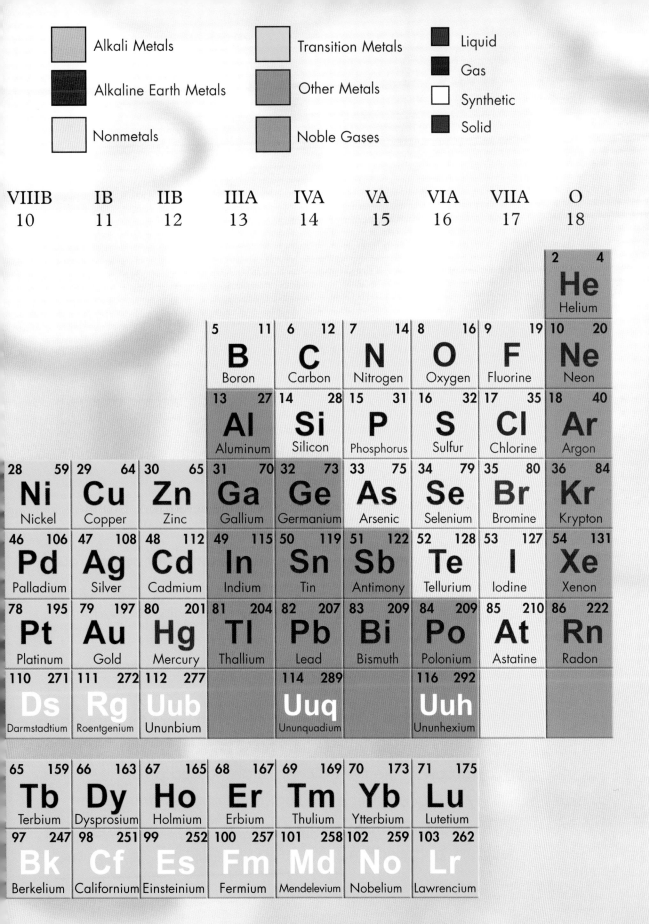

# Glossary

**atom** Smallest, most basic unit of an element, made up of protons, neutrons, and electrons.

**atomic number** Number of protons in the nucleus of an atom.

**atomic weight** Average mass of one atom of an element.

**bond** Force that holds two things together.

**compound** Substance made up of two or more elements.

**covalent bond** Chemical bond created when atoms share electrons.

**diatomic** Consisting of two atoms.

**electrolysis** Chemical change caused by passing an electric charge through water or other nonmetal substance.

**electron** Negatively charged particle outside the nucleus of an atom.

**element** Matter made up of one kind of atom.

**halogens** A family of elements, including fluorine, chlorine, bromine, iodine, and astatine.

**isotopes** Atoms of an element having the same number of protons but a different number of neutrons.

**molecule** Smallest particle of a substance that retains the properties of the substance and is composed of one or more atoms.

**nucleus** Core of an atom, containing protons and—except in the case of hydrogen—neutrons.

**neutron** Subatomic particle within the nucleus of an atom that has no charge; found in the nucleus of all elements except hydrogen.

**period** Horizontal row in the periodic table; also called a row.

**proton** Positively charged particle located in the nucleus of an atom.

**subatomic particles** Particles smaller than an atom, including protons, neutrons, and electrons.

Chlorine Chemistry Council
1300 Wilson Boulevard
Arlington, VA 22209
(703) 741-5000
Web site: http://www.C3.org

International Union of Pure and Applied Chemistry
IUPAC Secretariat
P.O. Box 13757
Research Triangle Park, NC 27709-3757
(919) 485-8700
Web site: http://www.iupac.org

The Salt Institute
700 N. Fairfax Street, Suite 600
Fairfax Plaza
Alexandria, VA 22314
(703) 549-4648
Web site: http://www.saltinstitute.org

## Web Sites

Due to the changing nature of Internet links, Rosen Publishing has developed an online list of Web sites related to the subject of this book. This site is updated regularly. Please use this link to access the list:

http://www.rosenlinks.com/uept/chlo

Atkins, P. W. *The Periodic Kingdom: A Journey into the Land of the Chemical Elements.* New York, NY: Basic Books, 1997.

Carson, Rachel. *Silent Spring.* 40th Anniversary ed. New York, NY: Houghton Mifflin, 2002.

Cobb, Cathy, and Monty L. Fetterolf. *The Joy of Chemistry: The Amazing Science of Familiar Things.* Amherst, NY: Prometheus Books, 2005.

Kurlansky, Carl. *Salt: A World History.* New York, NY: Penguin Books, 2002.

Nelson, Robin. *From Sea to Salt.* Minneapolis, MN: Lerner Publications, 2003.

Oxlade, Chris. *Elements and Compounds* (Chemicals in Action). Portsmouth, NH: Heinemann Library, 2002.

Stwertka, Albert. *A Guide to the Elements.* 2nd ed. New York, NY: Oxford University Press, 2002.

Tocci, Salvatore. *Chlorine* (True Books: Elements). Danbury, CT: Children's Press, 2006.

# Bibliography

Argonne National Laboratory, EVS. "Human Health Fact Sheet: Chlorine." August 2005. Retrieved December 6, 2006 (http://www.ead.anl.gov/pub/doc/chlorine.pdf).

Bentor, Yinon. "Periodic Table: Chlorine." 2006. Retrieved November 22, 2006 (http://www.chemicalelements.com/elements/cl.html).

British Broadcasting Corporation. "Historic Figures: Sir Humphry Davy." Retrieved October 21, 2006 (http://www.bbc.co.uk/history/historic_figures/davy_humphrey.shtml).

Chemical Heritage Foundation. "Humphry Davy." 2005. Retrieved October 21, 2006 (http://www.chemheritage.org/classroom/chemach/electrochem/davy.html).

Chlorine Chemistry Council. "The Chlorine Tree." May 2004. Retrieved October 1, 2006 (http://www.chlorinetree.org/pages/flash.html).

Cobb, Cathy, and Monty L. Fetterolf. *The Joy of Chemistry: The Amazing Science of Familiar Things.* Amherst, NY: Prometheus Books, 2005.

Kingston Technical Software. "Sir Humphry Davy." August 1999. Retrieved November 22, 2006 (http://www.corrosion-doctors.org/Biographies/DavyBio.htm).

Le Moyne College Department of Chemistry. "Carl Wilhelm Scheele." 1997. Retrieved November 22, 2006 (http://web.lemoyne.edu/~GIUNTA/scheele.html).

Little, Annie. U.S. Fish and Wildlife Service. "A Recovery Milestone for Bald Eagles." 2000. Retrieved November 17, 2006 (http://www.fws.gov/Endangered/recovery/milestone_b.html).

Logan, R. H. "World of Chemistry: The Home Page of Ralph Logan. The Nature of the Co-Valent Bond." August 1997. Retrieved December 5, 2006 (http://members.aol.com/profchm/covalent.html).

National Geographic. *National Geographic Field Guide to the Birds of North America*. 4th ed. Washington, DC: National Geographic Society, 2002.

Natural Resources Defense Council. "The Story of *Silent Spring*." 1997. Retrieved November 17, 2006 (http://www.nrdc.org/health/pesticides/hcarson.asp).

Newton, David E. *Chemical Elements from Carbon to Krypton, Volume 1, A–F*. Farmington Hills, MI: The Gale Group, 1999.

The Salt Institute. "FAQs on Salt and the Salt Industry." 1998. Retrieved October 1, 2006 (http://www.saltinstitute.org/3.html).

Stwertka, Albert. *A Guide to the Elements*. 2nd ed. New York, NY: Oxford University Press, 2002.

U.S. Environmental Protection Agency. "Polychlorinated Biphenyls (PCBs)." April 2006. Retrieved November 22, 2006 (http://www.epa.gov/pcb/pubs/effects.html).

U.S. Fish and Wildlife Service. "The Bald Eagle Is Back!" 2000. Retrieved November 17, 2006 (http://www.fws.gov/r9extaff/eaglejuly2.html).

U.S. Fish and Wildlife Service. "Endangered Still Means There's Time." 2006. Retrieved November 17, 2006 (http://www.fws.gov/endangered/kids/index.html).

U.S. Fish and Wildlife Service. "Organochlorides." Retrieved November 17, 2006 (http://www.fws.gov/pacific/ecoservices/envicon/pim/reports/contaminantinfo/contaminants.html).

U.S. Geological Survey. "Resources on Isotopes, Periodic Table—Chlorine." January 2004. Retrieved December 6, 2006 (http://wwwrcamnl.wr.usgs.gov/isoig/period/cl_iig.html).

U.S. Geological Survey. "Where Is Earth's Water Located?" August 2006. Retrieved December 5, 2006 (http://ga.water.usgs.gov/edu/earthwherewater.html).

Williams, Linda D. *Chemistry Demystified.* New York, NY: McGraw-Hill, 2003.

Wong, Edward. "The Reach of War: Chemical Weapons." *New York Times.* August 21, 2006.

# About the Author

Born in Gary, Indiana, and currently residing in New Hampshire, Linda Saucerman is a nonfiction writer and journalist specializing in science, the environment, and educational publishing. Her other books in this series are *Hydrogen* and *Carbon*.

Saucerman's science writing has appeared in several Chicago-area newspapers, in school textbooks, and in The Nature Conservancy magazine. Her interests include anthropology, archaeology, herpetology, and ornithology. When she isn't writing, Saucerman enjoys hiking in the woods with her husband, Matt, and her dog, Cooper.

# Photo Credits

Cover, pp. 1, 11, 12, 19, 22, 24 (bottom), 38–39 by Tahara Anderson; p. 5 © Johnny Johnson/Animals Animals Earth Scenes; pp. 8, 27, 29 © Getty Images; p. 10 © Charles D. Winters/Photo Researchers, Inc.; p. 15 Library of Congress Prints and Photographs Division; p. 17 © Tass/Sovfoto. Photo by Yuri Mashkov; p. 24 (top) © Laguna Design/ Photo Researchers, Inc.; p. 26 © James Holmes/Photo Researchers, Inc.; p. 30 NOAA; p. 33 Mark Golebiowski; p. 35 Cindy Reiman; p. 37 Shutterstock.com.

**Designer:** Tahara Anderson; **Editor:** Christopher Roberts
**Photo Researcher:** Cindy Reiman